DOCTOR·WHO

THE DARKSMITH LEGACY

BBC CHILDREN'S BOOKS
Published by the Penguin Group
Penguin Books Ltd, 80 Strand, London, WC2R 0RL, England
Penguin Group (USA) Inc., 375 Hudson Street, New York 10014, USA
Penguin Books (Australia) Ltd, 250 Camberwell Road, Camberwell, Victoria 3124, Australia
(A division of Pearson Australia Group Pty Ltd)
Canada, India, New Zealand, South Africa
Published by BBC Children's Books, 2009
Text and design © Children's Character Books, 2009
Written by Justin Richards
Cover illustration by Peter McKinstry
10 9 8 7 6 5 4 3 2 1
BBC logo © BBC 1996. Doctor Who logo © BBC 2004. TARIDS image © BBC 1963.
Licensed by BBC Worldwide Limited.
BBC, DOCTOR WHO (word marks, logos and devices), and TARDIS are trademarks of the
British Broadcasting Corporation and are used under licence.
ISBN: 978-1-40590-513-8
Printed in Great Britain by Clays Ltd, St Ives plc

DOCTOR·WHO

THE DARKSMITH LEGACY

THE DUST OF AGES

BY JUSTIN RICHARDS

Book
1

The Darksmith adventure continues online. Log on to
the website, enter the special codes from your book
and enjoy games and exclusive content about
The Darksmith Legacy.

www.thedarksmithlegacy.com

Contents

Earthlight

The dead dust stirred in the Earthlight. Despite the fact there was no air, and there could be no breeze, the fine particles were swept up and spun round, floating lazily in front of Earth hanging low in the dark sky.

The dust had been thrown up by a sudden weight pressing into the ground. Anyone watching across the cold, grey, dead lunar landscape would have seen an upright blue box slowly materialise. It was the only splash of bright colour, other than planet Earth watching from above.

The TARDIS had arrived on the moon.

TARDIS Data Bank

The Moon

Planet Earth has only one Moon.

Age   = approx 4.5 billion years

Diameter   = 3,476 km

Distance from Earth   = approx 384,400 km

(light takes about 1½ seconds to get from the Moon to Earth)

The Moon was the only other world that humans had ever travelled to by the year 2010. Six of the American Apollo missions landed on to the Moon between 1969 and 1972. Astronaut Neil Armstrong from Apollo 11 was the first man on the Moon. He described stepping on to the moon as 'one small step for man, one giant leap for mankind.'

Because the Moon always keeps the same face turned towards Earth as it orbits, the far side of the Moon is never seen. This is called the 'dark side of the moon' although it isn't always dark.

As the Moon orbits Earth, the light of the sun and Earth's own shadow falling across it make the Moon appear to change shape from a thin crescent to a full disc. The changing shape is called the Phases of the Moon. The complete cycle takes 29.53 days — a lunar month.

The Moon's gravity is about 1/6 of Earth's. The force of gravity between the Moon and Earth causes the tides in Earth's oceans. The Moon has no real oceans, though the flatter areas have names like *The Sea of Tranquillity*. But there is no water, no air and

Deep below the grey dusty surface, Clinton Seymour checked the readings on the controls he was monitoring. He reached for a microphone.

'Professor Dollund? We have an arrival. Just turned up in Sector 8.'

The professor's gruff voice echoed through a speaker in the control panel. 'Why didn't you warn me?'

'Sorry, sir. Didn't see him coming. It's like…' Seymour gave a short laugh. 'It's like the ship just faded into existence up there. Funny-looking craft, actually.'

Professor Dollund was not amused. 'Well, don't keep them hanging around. They could be important. Especially if they've got shielding – that suggests military. Give them a bubble.'

'Doing it now,' Seymour confirmed as he adjusted a control. The main screen in front of him showed a graphic of the lunar surface. An empty rectangular box rested on the landscape. As Seymour worked, a new line bulged up from the landscape, arcing upwards in a semi circle as it formed a large bubble over the box.

'OK, whoever you are,' Seymour said quietly. 'You've got air.'

The Doctor stood outside the TARDIS and looked up at Earth.

'Well, I was close,' he said. 'Wonder what drew the TARDIS off course.' He took a deep breath of impossible air and smacked his lips together in appreciation. 'Loads of questions,' he told himself. 'Absolutely loads.'

He turned in a full circle, his feet kicking up dust and coating his sneakers grey. 'This way,' he decided. He walked carefully, in a bouncing, skimming motion. The Moon's low gravity meant he only weighed a sixth of what he did on Earth.

The Doctor had gone about twenty paces when he hit the wall. It was hard, and smooth, and invisible. 'Or maybe not this way,' he said indistinctly, rubbing his nose. He stepped back and kicked a smattering of dust in the air, watching as the line of the wall was picked out in grey particles.

'Force bubble,' the Doctor decided. 'Might be for my benefit.' Just in case it was, he shouted, 'Thank you – much appreciated!'

As if in reply, a square of black opened in the ground a few metres away. He could just make out metal steps leading down into the darkness.

Lights snapped on as the Doctor started down the steps. His feet clanged on the metal, and he could feel himself getting heavier. He must be walking down into an artificial gravity field.

By the time he reached the bottom, the Doctor was back to his normal Earth weight. He was not surprised to find that there were people waiting for him.

There was a middle-aged man with grey hair, and a young woman whose long blonde hair was tied in a pony tail. Both were wearing dusty overalls.

'Welcome to Survey Four,' the man said.

'Thanks.' The Doctor grinned.

'We weren't expecting you,' the young woman confessed.

'That's all right. Unannounced inspection,' the Doctor said. 'You're not supposed to expect me.' He flashed his wallet of psychic paper, knowing it would tell them he was some important official.

The man swallowed as he read what he saw on the paper. 'Doctor Smith, from the Bureau of Alien Technology.'

'How did you know?' the woman asked nervously.

'We know everything,' the Doctor told her.

He tapped the side of his nose and winked. 'Absolutely everything. So you'd better leave nothing out when you tell me all about it. Start at the beginning, go on to the end, then stop. And assume I know nothing at all about who you are or what you're doing here on the Moon.'

The woman's name was Bobby (short for Roberta) Goodman, and she was an archaeologist. The man was Professor Dollund, and he told the Doctor he was in charge of Survey Four.

'Surveying what?' the Doctor asked. 'Assume I know nothing, remember,' he added quickly.

Dollund led the Doctor through narrow metal-lined corridors as he explained. 'With such a shortage of minerals and metal ores back on Earth, the big corporations think it's worth mining the Moon.'

'So you're surveying possible sites for the mines,' the Doctor realized.

'And turning up some interesting stuff,' Bobby said. 'Though nothing alien. At least, not until now.'

'Bobby's here to keep you people happy, really,' Dollund said. 'They wanted an expert ready on site, just in case.'

'You can never be too careful,' the Doctor agreed cheerfully. He noticed that Bobby and the professor exchanged glances.

'You'd better come into the main control room and see what we've found,' Dollund said.

He led the Doctor and Bobby along another corridor which ended in a large circular door. There was a big locking wheel in the middle of it. An airlock.

'Just a precaution,' Bobby said. 'There's some minor seismic activity in this area. If we get an earthquake it might rupture the seal on one of the tunnels.'

'You should call it a Moonquake. Why not use force bubbles, like you extruded on the surface for me?' the Doctor asked as he stepped into the large control room.

There was a young man sitting at the main control desk. He stood up as the Doctor entered.

'Force bubbles take too much power,' the young man said, hearing the Doctor's question. 'I've already deflated the one round your ship and recycled the air into the main tunnels.'

'Good idea,' the Doctor said cheerily. But he knew that meant he couldn't get back to the TARDIS. He was stuck here, until Goodman and her friends decided he could leave. Hopefully, that wouldn't be a problem.

The young man introduced himself as Clinton Seymour, the chief technician. He beckoned the Doctor over and showed him the main screen.

'Here it is,' he said. 'This green light is the problem.'

The screen showed a green light blinking on and off. Three blue lines pointed down at different angles. As the Doctor watched he saw that the lines were moving very slowly towards the light.

'Those are the robot drills,' Seymour explained.

One of the lines was almost touching the light. It was labelled 'Drill B', and like the others the speed of the drill was given along with more information.

'Drill B will get there first,' Bobby said.

'I don't think so,' the Doctor replied, and he told them why.

Activity

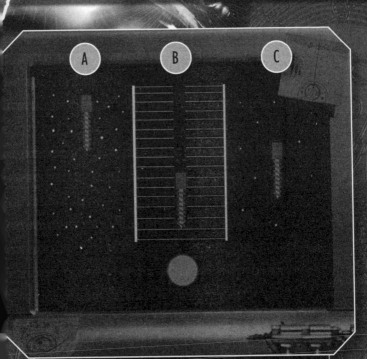

Rock Type

- Drill A - Hard-packed dust layer
- Drill B - Heavy rock formation
- Drill C - Loose dust

- **Drill A** Distance to Objective = 55 metres
  Speed = 1 metre per second

- **Drill B** Distance to Objective = 10 metres
  Speed = 0.5 metres per second

- **Drill C** Distance to Objective = 30 metres
  Speed = 10 metres per second

Which Drill Will Reach Objective First?
Computing Answer:

'The tunnels are automatically checked for leaks and pressurised as they're dug,' Dollund said. 'As soon as a drill reaches it, we can go and see what we've got.'

'And what have we got?' the Doctor asked.

'Who knows,' Bobby said. 'Power source of some kind. Henderson, he's the chief mining engineer, wondered if it might be a large deposit of quartz.'

'It is crystalline,' Dollund said. 'We can tell that at least.'

The line on the screen touched the light, and a message flashed up:

Objective Reached by Drill C

'You see, I was right,' the Doctor said. He was checking some of the readings on the other controls. 'I don't think it's natural, whatever it is. Certainly not quartz. Could be what drew the TARDIS off course,' he added quietly.

'Good job we have someone from the Bureau of Alien Technology here,' Dollund said.

'Isn't it,' the Doctor murmured. 'Isn't it just.'

Seymour reached for a microphone extending from the console on a flexible stalk. 'Henderson, what have you got down there?'

There was a crackle of static from the speakers, then a man's voice replied.

'It's incredible. Some sort of chamber. The drill's broken through into a vast cavern. Looks like whatever is down here is buried under the dust. Bobby – you there?'

'I'm here,' she replied. 'What is it?'

'I don't want to use the drill, we might damage whatever it is. I suggest you bring along your bag of tricks.'

'Good idea,' Bobby replied. 'We'll do this the old-fashioned way.'

'What's the old-fashioned way?' the Doctor wondered as the speaker clicked off.

'Trowel and brush. Standard archaeology,' Bobby told him.

'After all,' Dollund said, 'we have no idea what's really down there.'

'No,' the Doctor agreed. 'No idea at all.' He grinned at the professor. 'Exciting, isn't it?!'

Across
the Abyss

'You'd better stay here and keep an eye on things,' Professor Dollund said to Clinton Seymour.

'Will do,' the young man replied. 'If you need anything, give me a shout.'

Bobby led the way out of the control room and down a narrow corridor to what looked like the doors to a lift. She pressed a button, and the doors opened.

Inside was a small metal chamber, just big enough for the Doctor, Bobby and Professor Dollund to squeeze inside.

'This is cosy,' the Doctor remarked.

'Elevator capsule,' Dollund explained. 'It will take us to the bottom of the main shaft.'

'And what then?'

'Then we have to walk through the tunnels we've drilled,' Bobby said. 'Won't take long.

Don't worry, they're all air tight.'

'I wasn't worried,' the Doctor assured her, grinning. 'I don't worry. Well, not often. Should I be worried?' he checked.

Bobby didn't answer. She pressed a button on the wall and the elevator capsule dropped quickly down the shaft.

'What if we get stuck?' the Doctor asked cheerfully.

'There's a maze of tunnels criss-crossing the whole of this area,' Bobby told him. 'It would take a while, but we'd be able to walk back up to the main living area near the surface.'

'Assuming we could get out of this tin can,' the Doctor said, rapping his knuckles on the metal wall.

After a few more seconds, the elevator capsule slowed and then stopped. The doors slid open to reveal a tunnel. It had been cut from the rock, the walls were craggy and uneven. A line of puddles of light stretched into the distance. Every so often there was a metal bracing beam across the ceiling of the tunnel, holding the roof up. Each of the struts had a spotlight fixed to it, shining down at the tunnel floor.

'This takes us to a natural fissure,' Professor Dollund said. 'It's about a fifteen minute walk from there to the drill shaft.'

'And then it's down hill all the way,' the Doctor said.

'Shouldn't be too steep,' Bobby told him.

He nodded. 'Still, wish I'd brought my roller skates.'

The tunnel sloped down very gently, and after a while turned slowly to the left. Finally, it opened out into a wide ravine, the roof so high the Doctor couldn't even see it. There were lights fixed to the ragged walls to guide them.

Bobby led the way through the ravine. She stopped when she reached a part where the side walls disappeared. In front of them was a sheer drop into a deep abyss. A narrow strip of rock extended across to the other side, where the ravine continued.

'Not much of a bridge,' the Doctor observed.

'Best we can do, I'm afraid,' Bobby said. 'At least we don't have to lug all the equipment down here. Henderson and his assistant Lisa sent that down in a pod attached to the drill.'

'I'll go first,' Professor Dollund said. He was holding a device that looked a bit like a pocket calculator. 'The readings say it will take our weight.'

'Haven't you been across here before?' the Doctor asked.

'No need,' Dollund said. 'The drills have only just got past this point. It's only been vacuum-sealed for a few minutes. We're lucky to have the gravity at Earth normal.' He put one foot on the bridge.

The Doctor was frowning. 'You mean you've only this minute adjusted the gravity in this area?'

'What's the matter?' Bobby asked. 'Feeling light-headed?'

There was a clatter of stones falling into the abyss. The professor paused half way across the bridge. 'Actually, it doesn't feel that stable,' he said.

'Get across now!' the Doctor yelled. 'Don't dawdle – just run.'

'What?'

'Run!'

The professor looked confused, but he hurried across the narrow rock bridge. He had almost got to the other side when there was a tremendous cracking sound, and the rock split across the middle. The two pieces of bridge toppled into the abyss. The professor flung himself forwards, just managing to grab hold of the edge of the tunnel floor.

'Don't look down,' Bobby shouted as the professor clung desperately to the edge. 'Can you pull yourself up?'

The professor's hands were slipping. His fingers were losing their grip.

The Doctor pulled his coat off, bundled it into a ball and flung it across the gap.

'How's that help?' Bobby demanded.

'It doesn't,' he told her. 'But this does.' He backed up along the tunnel. Then he started to run.

'Doctor – you'll never make it!' Bobby yelled.

The Doctor reached the edge and leaped into space. His legs were still running, his arms flailing. He crashed into the far side of the abyss, close to where the professor was dangling. But the Doctor was slightly higher, his hands had a better grip and he managed to haul himself up into the tunnel. Then he reached down and grabbed the professor's hands, dragging him up too.

'Thank you, Doctor,' the professor gasped. 'What went wrong? The readings said it would be OK.'

'Yes,' the Doctor said. 'But they assumed lunar gravity – which is one sixth of Earth's. And now you've adjusted it to Earth normal.'

The professor nodded. 'So I weighed six times as much as the readings were assuming.'

'Too much for the bridge to hold,' the Doctor agreed.

'So how do I get over there?' Bobby called. 'I'm

not jumping – you only just made it.'

'Oh it'll be easy for you,' the Doctor called back. 'Tell Clinton to lower the gravity to lunar levels again, just till you're across. It's a simple jump at one sixth normal gravity.'

He was right. With the gravity reduced, Bobby made the jump easily – landing several metres further down the tunnel.

'Wahey!' she exclaimed. 'That was fun.'

'Better put the gravity back to Earth normal though,' the Doctor said. 'Otherwise we'll be bouncing about when we walk and banging our heads on the ceiling.'

They completed the journey without further incident. The ravine became narrower and lower, and finally they found themselves in an open area where the drill had been set up.

Cables and pipes snaked down a shallow incline where the drill had done its work. The path it had gouged out of the rock and dust was almost circular, and they had to walk down in single file. The slope wasn't too steep, but even so they had to be careful not to slip or to bump into each other as they went. Lights were strung up on a cable that was riveted to the roof.

'Not far now,' Bobby called back over her shoulder.

The Doctor was at the back, behind the professor, and he paused to examine the tunnel wall. It wasn't hard rock like earlier, but compacted dust. He drew his finger along the uneven surface and it came away coated with fine grey powder.

'Wouldn't like to have to spring clean down here,' he murmured, before hurrying to catch up.

The tunnel became shallower as they reached the end, and opened into a vast cavern. The roof was so high up the light didn't reach it.

The Doctor whistled. 'This is impressive.'

'Must be a natural formation,' Bobby said. 'Have you ever seen anything like it?'

'Can't say I have,' the professor said.

'Oh loads of times,' the Doctor told them. 'No, no – you go ahead and gawp. Enjoy yourselves. But I've done this sort of thing before. Impressive, but not unique.'

The cavern was lit by lamps that stood on metal tripods at intervals. There were two figures in the distance, pushing one of the large tripods into an upright position and adjusting the light on the top.

'There's Henderson,' Bobby said. 'And Lisa.'

'Lisa Summerton is our junior engineer,' the professor told the Doctor. 'Come and meet them. Let's see what they've found.'

Henderson was a short man with an impressive moustache. His dark hair was streaked with grey – though whether that was because of his age or from the dust that was everywhere, the Doctor couldn't tell.

Lisa Summerton had close-cropped hair, and the Doctor could see a tattoo of a butterfly on her arm where her short-sleeved overalls ended. Both the engineers looked hot from their work.

'This is it,' Henderson said, leading them over to one wall of the cavern. 'The drill broke through into this chamber, and we've sent all three drills back up shaft A by remote control.'

Lisa had a device similar to the one the professor had used to check the rock bridge. She held it in front of the wall of the cavern. 'The energy source, whatever it is, seems to be less than a metre behind this wall.'

'May I?' The Doctor took the device from her and examined the readings. He tapped the screen, shook the device, held it sideways and squinted at it through his glasses. Then he licked it. 'I think you're right,' he agreed. 'And it does seem to be crystalline, doesn't it. And definitely alien,' he added.

'I'm sorry,' Lisa said, taking back her device. 'But who are you?'

'He's from the Bureau of Alien Technology,' Professor Dollund said.

'From BAT?' Henderson was impressed.

'Which I guess makes me the BAT man,' the Doctor said with a grin. 'But you can just call me the Doctor.'

'So what do you think it is, Doctor?' Bobby asked.

The Doctor examined the wall. He tapped it and rubbed at it. Grey dust flaked off and fell to the floor.

'I have your tools here, Bobby,' Lisa said. She pointed to a large rucksack lying nearby.

'Thanks. I'll get a brush and a trowel,' Bobby said.

'You know, I don't think that'll be necessary,' the Doctor told her. He was digging his hands into the wall and gouging out handfuls of the grey dust. 'It's just coming away, look. Soon see what's inside… Like a lucky dip, or a bran tub – you ever done that? Oh.'

The Doctor was standing absolutely still, staring at the wall where he had been working.

'What is it, Doctor?' the professor asked.

'Well...' The Doctor stepped back so they could all see.

The wall was a grey mass, hollowed out where the Doctor had been scooping out the dust.

And from the middle of the hollow something was poking out into the cavern.

'Is that what I think it is?' Lisa asked nervously.

'I'm afraid so,' the Doctor said. 'It's a hand. A human hand.'

The Secret of the Cavern

Nervously, Bobby reached out and touched the hand that was poking out of the grey wall of dust. It was cold, like stone.

'It isn't real,' she said. 'It's a statue or something.'

'Well, that's a relief,' the Doctor said, grinning.

'You knew, didn't you?'

'Knew it wasn't anyone I'd met,' he said. 'Though there is something familiar about the fingernails.'

'It's exquisitely carved,' Professor Dollund said. He leaned forward to peer at the hand. 'Is it stone, do you suppose?'

'Careful,' Bobby said, as the professor tapped at the back of the hand with his fingertips.

There was a loud crack, and the hand dropped away, sheared off at the wrist. With lightning-fast reactions, the Doctor caught it before it hit the ground.

'That was…' Lisa said, impressed.

'Handy?' the Doctor finished for her. 'Here you go.' He gave the broken hand to Bobby.

'I need to get this preserved,' she said. 'I've got a specimen box in my toolkit. I'd like to get it back to the main base and run an analysis. I'd like to fetch some equipment too. This wall is so soft I think a vacuum hose would be more use and do less damage than a brush and trowel.'

'Is there a different way back?' Dollund asked Henderson. 'We had a bit of bother on the way down here.'

'What happened?'

'Oh nothing much,' the Doctor told him. 'Collapsing rock bridge, possible fall into bottomless crevasse, long jump over the abyss. Usual sort of thing, really.'

Henderson and Lisa looked at him, neither sure if he was joking or serious.

'So another way back would be useful,' the professor prompted.

'Oh, yes,' Henderson said. 'We can take the secondary shaft. It's a bit further but it'll get us back to the elevator capsule a different way.'

Bobby opened her rucksack and rummaged around inside. She pulled out a clear plastic box.

'Sandwiches?' the Doctor asked.

But she didn't answer. She opened the lid and put the hand inside. It almost filled the box. 'It's not air tight,' she explained. 'But it will do until we can get the hand up to the control room.'

'I'll take it back to Clinton, and he can start analysing it,' Professor Dollund said. 'You can make a start down here. We still haven't found that energy source.'

'Oh, it's in there somewhere,' the Doctor told him. 'Tell you what, I'll come with you. I could do with a bit of exercise, and you can explain a bit more about what you're up to here and how your survey is going.'

'I'll be glad of the company, to tell you the truth,' Dollund agreed. He pushed the box with the hand into his own rucksack and swung it up on to his back.

'We'll make a start,' Bobby said. 'We can brush away some of the surface dust and dirt. But if you can bring back the vacuum hoses, that'll be a big help.'

The journey passed quickly with Professor Dollund giving the Doctor rather more detail than he wanted about the survey. In fact, the Doctor was more interested in what Clinton Seymour's analysis of the broken hand would say, but he didn't tell the professor that.

They soon arrived back at the elevator capsule, arriving from a tunnel on the other side of it this time. The journey had indeed been longer, but a much easier walk through gently sloping tunnels with rough rock walls.

Bobby had called ahead to tell Clinton what was happening, and the young technician was waiting for them when the capsule arrived back in the main base. He led them back to the main control room.

'Can't wait to get a look at this hand thing,' Clinton said. 'I've set things up so we can run a few tests. Spectrographic analysis and that sort of thing. Carbon dating too. With luck we can find out what it's made of and how old it is.'

'The hand is in here,' Professor Dollund said, swinging his rucksack off his back and setting it down on a workbench at the side of the room. He unzipped the rucksack, and lifted out the clear plastic box.

It was empty.

The Doctor and Dollund stared at the box.

'Well, where is it?' Clinton asked, not realising anything was wrong. He reached into the rucksack and felt round inside. 'Just dust in here. The stuff gets everywhere.'

'It's gone,' Dollund said, shaking his head in disbelief. 'It was in there. In that box.'

'What?' Clinton said.

'He's right,' the Doctor confirmed. 'Bobby put the hand in the box, and the professor put it in his rucksack. No one has taken it out, and the box was sealed. Now it's empty.'

'Well, apart from some dust,' Clinton said, staring into the box. 'I told you, it gets everywhere.'

'Never mind the dust,' Professor Dollund protested. 'What's happened to the hand?'

Before anyone could answer, there was a bleeping sound from the main control console.

'That's Bobby calling in,' Clinton said, hurrying to operate a control. 'Clinton here. You'll never guess what's happened.'

'Never mind that.' Bobby's voice was clear and

loud through the speakers. 'Is the Doctor there?'

'I'm here,' he replied. 'What is it?'

'We were talking, discussing how best to approach the excavation without damaging whatever is inside the rock and dust. It's obviously fragile.'

'Obviously,' the Doctor said. He had his glasses on and was examining the almost empty plastic box.

'So we were looking through my tools, waiting for those vacuum hoses. Then we went back to look again at the wall…' Her voice tailed off.

'And?' the Doctor prompted. 'What did you find?'

'We found the hand,' Bobby said. 'The hand you took with you. It's back. Sticking out of the wall, just like it was before.'

'That's good,' the Doctor said slowly.

'Good? Why is that good?'

'Because we were sort of wondering where it had gone,' the Doctor said. 'Don't touch anything. We'll be back with those vacuum hoses in two shakes of a lamb's tail. Actually, make that three shakes. We'll come the long way again.'

The vacuum hoses were thick plastic tubes connected to a small metal cylinder. Dust was sucked through the tubes, and sprayed out of a hole at the back of the cylinder.

Bobby set to work with one of the hoses, working her way carefully round the hand that once again extended from the wall of dust and dirt. Professor Dollund and Lisa watched while Henderson adjusted controls on the cylinder.

Beside her, the Doctor was peering through his glasses, pointing to areas he wanted uncovered. It was a slow job, but before long they had removed enough of the wall to reveal that the hand was attached to a wrist. And an arm.

'How extraordinary,' Professor Dollund said. 'It must have been here for centuries, yet this statue, or whatever it will turn out to be, seems human. And it seems to be wearing a suit.'

They took it in turns to operate the hoses, gradually uncovering more and more of the figure embedded in the wall of the enormous cavern. A grey statue, exactly the same colour and texture as the Moon dust around it, but hard as coal.

'Here's something else,' Lisa said. She was moving the hose gently across the figure's chest. On its lowest setting it was gently sucking dust and debris from where the man's tie would be.

But instead something glittered as it caught the light. Something about the size and shape of an egg, but faceted like a jewel.

'Crystalline,' Professor Dollund said. 'That could be our energy source. We should call Clinton up in the control room and see if he's getting a stronger reading.'

'In a minute,' Bobby said. 'See if you can get it free first.'

'I wouldn't try,' Henderson said as Lisa gently tugged at the transparent crystal. 'We've been excavating from the bottom of the wall, disturb it too much too suddenly and the whole lot could come down.'

'Like taking a tin of beans from the bottom of the pile,' the Doctor said. 'I've tried that. Not recommended.'

'I think it's coming,' Lisa said. 'Just give me a second.'

But she didn't have a second. With a sudden roar, the whole side of the wall above her slipped and collapsed. The Doctor grabbed Lisa's arm, dragging her clear as dust and soil and rock avalanched down.

They stood coughing and spluttering as the dust slowly settled. The light struggled through as the air cleared, revealing the statue standing in front of them, free of the wall at last. For the first time, they could see its head. They could see its face.

'That's not possible,' Bobby gasped, wiping dust from her eyes and blinking at the grey figure in front of them.

'No wonder that hand looked a bit familiar,' the Doctor said quietly.

The figure standing in front of them – the figure made of dusty rock that had been buried for centuries – stared back impassively. With the Doctor now coated with grey dust, it was like looking in a mirror.

The statue was wearing a suit. It had spiky hair and thin features. Except for the crystal gleaming at its throat, it was the exact image of the Doctor.

The Hand of Fear

Clinton Seymour watched the energy readings change. They increased slightly and he guessed that Bobby and the others had uncovered the power source – whatever it was.

There was a thin layer of fine dust across the top of the main console where he was working. He brushed it away with the back of his hand.

The communicator beeped, and Clinton answered. 'Hey there – what's going on? The power source readings are increasing. You found something?'

'You could say that,' Henderson's voice replied. 'We've used the vacuum hoses to uncover what seems to be a statue.'

'Cool!' Clinton said. 'It must have been buried there for centuries.'

'The thing is,' Henderson went on, 'this statue… well – it's a statue of the Doctor.'

'What?' There was another thin layer of fine dust across the top of the main console, and Clinton again brushed it away with the back of his hand. 'But that's impossible.'

'Isn't it just?' the Doctor's voice answered. 'It's a good likeness though. I'm very pleased with it. Looking good.'

Yet another thin layer of fine dust had appeared across the top of the console. Irritated, Clinton swept it away once more. Then he frowned, realising he had already done this twice before. 'That's odd,' he said.

'What? Something to do with the readings you're getting?' the Doctor asked.

'No, nothing like that.' Clinton swivelled in his chair to look at the floor where he'd swept the dust. 'The dust…' He stopped, staring open-mouthed.

The floor was covered in a layer of grey dust. It was deeper by the side of the console and close to the door. Clinton looked up, wondering if it was falling from the ceiling. 'How did that happen?'

'How did what happen?' the Doctor's voice demanded through the speakers. 'Clinton – what's going on up there?'

'Oh nothing. Nothing to worry about. Just…' He gasped in astonishment as he looked back at the dusty floor. 'OK, now I'm worried.'

'What is it?'

'Doctor – that hand, the one that disappeared? It's back.'

Bobby was frowning. 'What's he mean?'

'I don't know,' the Doctor said.

Before he could ask, there was a shout of surprise and fear from the intercom.

'Clinton – Clinton are you all right?' Henderson shouted.

The shout had subsided to a retching, gasping sound. The Doctor was running across the cavern. Henderson hurried after him.

'It might be quicker to take the access tunnel,' he shouted as he caught the Doctor up. 'If we run.'

'How long?'

Henderson had a device like a calculator, except on its screen it showed a schematic map of the tunnels and the base. He examined the screen, holding it so the Doctor could see.

Activity

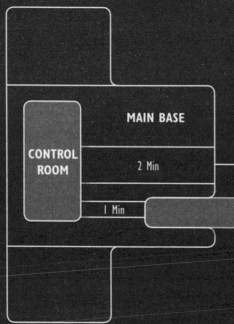

MAIN BASE

CONTROL ROOM

2 Min

1 Min

Distances:

Cavern to elevator capsule – – – – – – – – – –	5 Minutes
Bottom of elevator shaft to arrival point in main base –	3 Minutes
Elevator arrival in base to main control – – – – – –	2 Minutes
From cavern to access tunnel – – – – – – – – –	1 Minute
From start of access tunnel to main base – – – – –	6 minutes
From access tunnel entry to base to control room – –	1 Minute

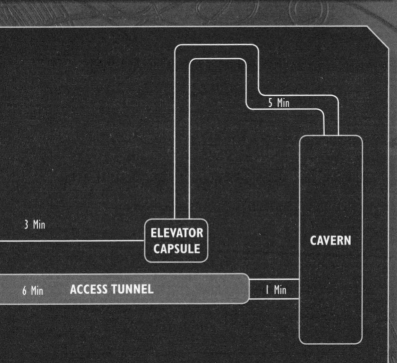

3 Min

ELEVATOR CAPSULE

5 Min

CAVERN

6 Min **ACCESS TUNNEL**

1 Min

Which route is quickest? Computing Answer...

'Then the answer's obvious,' the Doctor said, as they ran. 'Lead the way!'

The grey hand from the statue was lying on the floor when Clinton saw it. He had been speaking to the Doctor on the intercom, at the same time stooping down to examine the hand.

He had reached out, carefully, nervously, towards it.

And the hand *jumped*. It suddenly extended its fingers, propelling itself at Clinton's face.

That was when he cried out. The hand was clamped to his face, cutting off his breathing. He scrabbled at it, trying to tear it away. He managed to lever the finger away from his bruised cheeks. But the hand dropped slightly and the fingers curled round his throat, choking him.

Clinton was pulling at it with both his own hands. The hand was cold and hard as stone, clamped on his windpipe. He managed to work his fingers underneath. His vision was blurring and misty. With a last, desperate effort, he prised the hand away from his neck, and hurled it away.

The hand clattered to the floor. Its fingers scrabbled in the dust. It dragged itself along by its fingertips, heading back towards Clinton. Bracing itself, ready to jump again.

Clinton was looking around, trying to find anything he could use to defend himself. How did the thing know where he was – could it see him? Hear him? Maybe it could *smell* him? He backed away behind the main console, trying to hide.

How long he stayed silent and still, crouched behind the console, he didn't know. Was help coming? Was the hand still there – still hunting for him?

He caught a slight movement out of the corner of his eye. Something grey shimmered as it caught the light. But it was only dust, blowing as if in a slight breeze. Cautiously, Clinton stood up. He looked around carefully, peering into any shadow or corner where the hand might be hiding.

But he didn't see it until it leaped.

With a gasp of astonishment, Clinton grabbed the nearest thing to defend himself with – the chair beside the console. It was heavy, but he was desperate. He swung the chair in a low arc, right at the hand.

The hand and the chair met with an impact that jarred Clinton's arms. He dropped the chair.

The hand exploded into a cloud of dust. Clinton sank to his knees.

At the same moment the door opened and the Doctor sprinted in, skidding across the dusty floor and stopping right in front of Clinton. Henderson appeared in the doorway behind him, looking hot and flustered.

'We got here as fast as we could,' he said breathlessly. 'Took the access tunnel and ran all the way. Now, what seems to be the problem?'

But before Clinton could answer, the intercom beeped and Lisa's voice came out of the speakers.

'Doctor? Are you there yet? Is everything OK?'

'We're fine,' the Doctor called. 'And Clinton's fine too, I think. Just going to tell us all about it.'

'Before he does,' Lisa said, 'there's something you should know. While we were worrying about Clinton, something happened to the statue.'

'Let me guess,' Clinton said. 'Its hand's gone missing again?'

'No, stranger than that. It's *changed*.'

'Changed?' the Doctor said. 'What do you mean, *changed*?'

'I mean it doesn't look like you any more.'

'No accounting for taste,' the Doctor muttered.

Louder he said, 'So, what does it look like?'

It was Bobby's voice that answered. 'It's still got that crystal in the same place. But the whole figure is different. I don't understand it. Like Lisa said, it doesn't look like you, Doctor. It looks exactly like *me*.'

Half a galaxy away, on the cold desolate planet Karagula, a meeting was taking place. Three figures stood in the central chamber of a vast, sprawling stone edifice. From the outside it looked like a gigantic medieval cathedral. Set on a rocky plain, built into the side of a mountain it looked like it might have grown there rather than been built.

The high, vaulted ceiling of the chamber was held up by enormous carved pillars. The conference table in the centre of the room was like a giant stone altar. The sign of the dark flame was embossed on its sides and on its top surface.

The three figures all wore heavy, dark, hooded cloaks. One was a deep crimson, another purple, the third grey.

The grey figure spoke. Its voice was like the brittle, flaking stone that made up the floor and walls. 'You are sure it is the Crystal, Brother Talen?'

The crimson-cloaked figure nodded. 'There can be no mistake. After all these years, it has been found.'

· 'We are homing in on the location now,' the purple-cloaked figure said. 'It is somewhere in Mutter's Spiral. Soon we will know the star system, and then the exact position.'

'Thank you, Sister Hellan. You have done well.'

High Minister Drakon, the leader of the Darksmith Collective folded back his dark grey hood. Beneath it, his hairless head was like a skull encased in amber. His pale yellow skin was translucent, the bone beneath clearly visible. Veins traced their way through the jelly-like flesh, throbbing and pumping.

'We have waited for centuries,' he said quietly. 'And now, the waiting is almost over.'

Escape to Danger

While Lisa and Bobby were talking on the intercom, Professor Dollund was examining the statue.

'It's extraordinary,' he said, peering at the grey face that was exactly like Bobby's. 'Absolutely extraordinary.'

'How can it have happened?' Lisa asked, joining him. Behind them Bobby was still talking to the Doctor.

'I wish I knew. Some sort of molecular rearrangement, perhaps. Maybe it's trying to find the most effective shape and form based on what it touches – first the Doctor, then you…' The professor stopped in surprise.

'Maybe we're about to find out,' Lisa said. 'Bobby – look at this.'

As they watched, the statue changed again. It started with the face. The features seemed to shimmer and blur. Dust rolled from the eyes like dry tears. The nose receded, and the whole face seemed to dissolve into a shapeless blob.

The same thing was happening to the rest of the figure. Details of the clothes became smudged and blurred. Then the limbs themselves dissolved.

Bobby was trying to explain what was happening over the intercom. But she stopped as the distorted shape in front of them started to move. A shapeless, dusty leg twitched, then slid forwards. Another lifted slightly, bending at the knee. The figure took a step towards the professor, Lisa and Bobby.

Grey arms reached out. Stubby fingers clutched the air, dust showering down from them. The creature took another shuffling step. Then one arm seemed to extend suddenly. A dry, dusty hand smothered Professor Dollund's face. Another dragged him towards the walking statue.

Lisa gave a shriek, grabbing the professor's arm and trying to pull him away. Bobby dropped the communicator as she rushed to help.

'What is it? What's going on?' the Doctor's voice demanded through the speakers.

Bobby and Lisa were struggling to drag the professor clear as the dusty creature engulfed him.

'We're on our way!' the Doctor was yelling.

With a horrible sucking sound, the professor's head came free of the creature's grip. He staggered backwards, almost falling. Bobby helped him keep his balance.

'Let's get out of here,' she said.

The three of them ran across the chamber, heading for the access tunnel. Behind them, the shapeless statue lumbered forward.

The wall behind the statue shimmered and bulged. Another shapeless approximation of a figure pulled itself out of the wall and lumbered after the first across the cavern…

The Doctor and Henderson hurried from the control room.

'Hey, you're not leaving me behind this time,' Clinton shouted after them. He set off at a run to catch them up.

Henderson led the way back to the access tunnel, and soon the three of them were running down the shallow incline.

The Doctor skidded to a halt so suddenly that Clinton and Henderson almost ran into him.

'Can you hear that?' the Doctor said, looking towards the point in front of them where the tunnel turned.

'What?' Henderson asked.

'Someone's coming,' Clinton said.

Sure enough, from ahead of them came the sound of rapid footsteps, echoing off the rock walls of the tunnel. Distorted shadows danced across the tunnel floor, as something moved in front of the wall-mounted lights in the next section of tunnel. It looked as if something huge and shapeless was oozing towards them.

'What is it?' Henderson gasped.

But then three figures appeared round the corner. Three human figures. Their shadows elongated and distorted by the angle of the lights behind them. Professor Dollund, Bobby and Lisa were running towards the Doctor and his friends.

'Thank goodness,' Dollund said. 'We have to get out of here.'

'Those things can't be far behind us,' Bobby said.

The Doctor looked at them with interest.

'Really? What things?'

'Horrible,' Lisa told him. 'The statue – it sort of came to life.'

'Shapeless creatures. They almost got the professor,' Bobby explained.

'One of them just came out of the wall of the cavern.'

'What?' Clinton said. 'But that's impossible. Isn't it, Doctor?' he asked, suddenly worried.

'Well, not if it happened,' the Doctor pointed out. 'Tell me, how did it happen? Did the rock wall sort of bulge out, then form into a shape that detached itself from the wall? A shape that then sort of grew legs to walk, and arms to reach out to get you?'

'Yes,' Bobby said. 'How did you guess?'

'I didn't,' the Doctor said. 'It's happening just over there.'

They whirled round, in time to see a massive shape heave itself out of the rock wall of the tunnel behind Lisa.

'Back to the base!' Clinton shouted.

They turned to run. But the walls of the tunnel behind them were bulging now. The rock was shimmering and rippling. Dust flaked to the floor.

The lights flickered and one of them went out. Then another. The rest were getting noticeably dimmer.

'Power's going,' Henderson said. 'If the oxygen pumps stop...' He didn't need to complete the thought.

He didn't have time either. 'Run!' the Doctor yelled. He pushed Professor Dollund ahead of him, and everyone charged up the tunnel.

A grey shape whipped at them. The floor was moving beneath them. Hands punched through the rock walls, clawing at them as they ran past.

Lisa screamed as something caught in her hair. But when she thumped at it, it was just dust.

Bobby struggled to keep her balance as the whole tunnel floor heaved and tilted. Henderson lashed out at the arms that stretched across the tunnel like a spider's web to try to catch him. Dollund was yelling for them all to hurry as he struggled past the grey limbs that clawed and thrashed at him. Clinton just put his head down and charged through, eyes closed.

The Doctor walked calmly after them. He slapped away a misshapen hand that reached for him. It exploded in a shower of dust.

'Fascinating,' he said quietly. He grinned

and shook his head. 'Extraordinary, but fascinating.' Then he realized that the grey shapes were getting thicker, stronger, faster and he dashed quickly after the others.

As soon as everyone was through, Henderson slammed shut the huge airtight hatch at the end of the access tunnel.

'The walls here are lined with metal, and will keep anything out.'

'Sure about that?' the Doctor asked. He brushed himself down, dust showering to the floor. He stamped his feet, hoping to get the dust off his trainers. 'These used to be white,' he complained. 'Now look at them. Still, they say grey is the new black. It's the new white now, too.'

The main lights flickered, and went out. Red emergency lighting cut in.

'Main generator's stopped,' Henderson said.

'Will we still have oxygen?' Dollund asked.

'So long as the backup emergency generator doesn't pack up too,' Clinton told him.

The Doctor was jumping up and down, dust flying round him as it shook off his clothes and shoes.

'What are you doing?' Bobby asked.

'Just checking the gravity. Seems OK for now.' He clapped his hands together. 'Right, I've got a sonic screwdriver, so let me at this generator of yours.'

'We can manage,' Henderson told him. 'It just needs resetting.'

'Happens every now and again,' Lisa said.

'Oh.' The Doctor sounded disappointed. 'OK, you sort it out then, and I'll…' He shrugged and stamped his feet some more. 'I'll come and watch maybe.'

'You can come with me, Doctor,' Clinton said. 'Once the main power's back we can send a signal to Moonport Five and get them to send help. We won't be able to boost a signal that far until the generator's back, but as soon as it is we can send a mayday.'

'They're overstretched as it is,' Dollund said. 'You really think they'll send help to a small operation like ours?'

'That's why I want the Doctor with me,' Clinton said.

'Of course,' Bobby realized. 'If an agent of the Bureau of Alien Technology asks for help, they're sure to send someone.'

'Er,' the Doctor said. 'Yes. Well.' He sighed, then grinned. 'Better get started then. Henderson – you and Lisa get us power as soon as you can.'

The main generator was controlled from a small room at the back of the main base. It was one of the first parts of the base to be constructed, hewn out of the Moon rock itself.

Henderson and Lisa had restarted the generator several times. It was old and temperamental, and as the base expanded and the tunnels grew it was less and less able to cope with the demands for power.

The door slid open and Henderson let Lisa go in first. She headed straight for the main control console, while Henderson went over to the enormous generator itself. Only the side of it extended into the room. The rest was built out into the Moon rock beyond.

'Diagnostics says the main filters are blocked,' Lisa reported.

'We cleaned them last week, didn't we?' Henderson set about taking off the grille of the generator. 'It shouldn't get clogged up that quickly.'

'I'm just telling you what it says. The filters are blocked so the air cooling isn't working. The system's cut out so it doesn't overheat.'

Henderson pulled out a long, rectangular filter. It should have been a fine plastic mesh, perhaps spotted with dirt trapped as the air circulated inside the generator. But the filter was completely coated with thick dust. Henderson coughed as the dust became a thick cloud.

'Where did that come from?' he managed to gasp. He reached in for another filter. 'They're all the same, look.'

'I'd love to,' Lisa said. 'But I can't see anything.'

The air was thick with dust. It drifted like smoke.

'We'd better find a vacuum hose and get them clean,' Henderson said. 'There must be a leak in the system where it's getting drawn in.'

There was no reply.

'Lisa?'

Henderson peered into the mist of dust hanging in the air. A dark shape was approaching him.

'Oh, there you are.'

But it wasn't Lisa. The figure was taller,

broader, darker. It wasn't a person at all, just an approximation of a human figure. A massive grey shape reaching through the dusty air for Henderson.

And from the other side of the room, somewhere beyond the dust, came Lisa's muffled screams.

Restart

The red emergency lighting was still on in the the main control room. It bathed everything and everyone blood red. Clinton was sitting at his console, checking readings.

'Generator's still out,' he reported.

'Doesn't usually take them this long to reset it,' Dollund said.

Bobby saw the Doctor's frown. 'You think there's a problem?'

'I think there are loads of problems. Masses of problems. Don't suppose you have a security camera or something in the generator room?' he asked Clinton.

'We do,' he said. 'But there's not enough power to run it without the generator.'

The Doctor sniffed. 'Good design. Who sold you that, then?'

'We can talk to them though.' Clinton pressed the communicator button. 'Henderson – how's it going down there?'

The speakers crackled with static.

'Henderson? Lisa?'

Still there was no answer.

'Something's not right. I'm going down there,' the Doctor said.

He ran from the room, then skidded to a halt, looking first one way then the other.

Bobby joined him. 'It's this way,' she said.

They ran through the base, dust swirling round their feet as they kicked it up. Soon they were outside the generator room. The door was shut.

'It won't open!' Bobby said, trying the controls.

'Let me.' The Doctor pointed his sonic screwdriver at the controls. The end glowed with a blue light and there was a flash followed by a shower of sparks. The door slid open.

The room looked as though it had been abandoned long ago. Everything was covered with a layer of dust. It could have been years since anyone had been inside. Except for the bodies.

Henderson was lying by the access panel to the generator. Lisa was slumped over the control console on the other side of the room. Like everything else, both were coated with dust.

'But they've only been here a few minutes,' Bobby said. 'Are they...?'

The Doctor was already examining Henderson. He ran over to check on Lisa.

'They'll be fine,' he said. 'Unconscious – almost suffocated.'

'But how?'

'Choking on dust, I should think.' The Doctor hauled Lisa out of her chair and carried her into the corridor. He put her down gently, propping her against a wall. Then he dragged Henderson after her.

'Can I do anything?'

'Check their airways are clear and make sure there's no dust in their mouths. I'll get the generator started.'

'Only Henderson and Lisa can do that,' Bobby said. 'It's a security measure. The computer prompts you and you have to know the next symbol in the sequence to reset the systems.'

The Doctor paused in the doorway. 'Can't be that hard to work out,' he said. 'And if I'm right, we need to get power back and get a message out as soon as we can. We're all in the most terrible danger.'

Bobby gave a nervous laugh. 'From this dust?'

But the Doctor was deadly serious. 'Yes. Dust that can clog up the communications so they won't work. Dust that can choke you, dust that can shape itself into walking statues to come after you and smother you. Dust that can kill.'

71

Activity

1. △△   2. |||| 3. ⊂   4. ⫽≠

Which symbol is next in the sequence?
Enter your Answer: _____

Which symbol is the odd one out?
Enter your Answer: _____

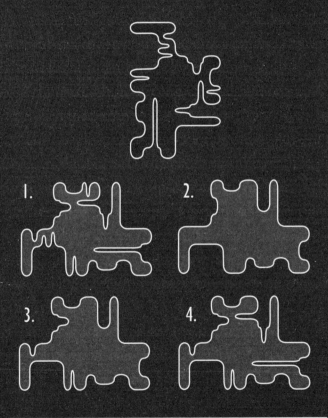

Which symbol fits the empty space?
Enter your Answer: _____

The Doctor answered the questions displayed on the computer screen on the console as quickly as he could. They weren't too difficult, and he suspected they were not for security as much as to confirm the operator really did want to reset the systems.

The next symbol in the sequence was obviously the third one. Or was it the second? No – definitely the third. But the odd one out, that was the second symbol. Then it was just a matter of finding the one that fitted the socket, like a key had to fit a lock. That was a bit trickier as they needed turning, and the Doctor found himself twisting his head round and squinting to work it out. He grinned, and selected the first of the possible symbols.

There was a satisfying whirring sound from behind him as the generator started up again. The red lights dimmed and were replaced by the harsh white light of the main systems.

The Doctor made some adjustments to the settings on the main console, then hurried to join Bobby in the corridor outside.

'I've set the generator's cooling system to use water instead of air. It's not as efficient, but the water cooling is a sealed system. With luck, the dust won't get in and clog it all up again.'

Henderson's eyelids were fluttering as he regained consciousness. 'That's very clever, Doctor,' he said weakly.

'How are you feeling?' Bobby asked.

'Terrible. My throat's so sore and dry.'

'That'll be the dust,' the Doctor said. He checked on Lisa and was pleased to see that she too was coming round.

As soon as they were strong enough, the Doctor and Bobby helped Henderson and Lisa to their feet.

'Let's get back to the main control room,' the Doctor said. 'Clinton needs to send that mayday message.'

'We should be fine now the power's back,' Bobby said.

'Don't bet on it,' the Doctor told her. 'Look!'

The corridor in front of them was filling with dust. It hung in the air, and swirled round their feet like a sandstorm. Slowly but surely, the dust was coming together to form shapes – huge, lumpy, grey figures that reached out for the Doctor and his friends...

On the distant planet of Karagula, High Minister

Drakon of the Darksmith Collective watched as a group of Brother technicians demonstrated their latest creation.

Brother Ardos was in charge of the project. He was dwarfed by the massive creature fashioned from plastic and metal that stood silently beside him. Almost two metres tall, it was in the shape of a man. Through the sections of transparent plastic, gears and levers, circuits and motors were visible. The whole robot gave an impression of colossal strength and power.

'We have used every last item of temporal engineering we have acquired over the years. Who knows what the Agent will be called upon to do in order to recover the Eternity Crystal. We have fashioned its body from the hardest metal augmented with plastics salvaged from the wreckage of the Nestene homeworld. It has been programmed with the innate understanding of the time Vortex that we found in a deactivated Gundan robot. Sister Clathine's forge has been working at full capacity to bring these elements together and fuse them with our own technologies and discoveries.'

Drakon nodded with approval. His skull-like face was twisted into what might have been a smile.

'You have done well. As soon as we have the exact location, we shall despatch the Agent with all speed to recover the Eternity Crystal.'

One of the cloaked figures standing nearby stepped forward. 'High Minister, I must question whether this is wise.'

Drakon turned slowly to face the Darksmith who had spoken. 'Brother Stemnos, you question the wisdom of the High Witan of the Darksmiths? You would rather leave the Eternity Crystal, and for the first time in our long history, fail to fulfil a contract?'

Stemnos took a step backwards. 'My apologies. I know that our clients are most insistent, and that they have become impatient over the years since the Crystal was lost. But this effort, this technology – surely the cost outweighs any payment we shall receive from the client for delivering the final device.'

'We must fulfil our contract, as we always have. And to do that we need the Crystal that Brother Varlos took from us when he fled from Karagula.' High Minister Drakon pointed at the large robot standing before them. 'Here we have the means to recover the Crystal and fulfil the contract. An Agent that can ride the time winds, that can destroy any opposition, that will stop at nothing to achieve its mission. The honour of the Darksmith Collective hangs in the balance. There is no power in the universe that can stop us from recovering the Eternity Crystal!'

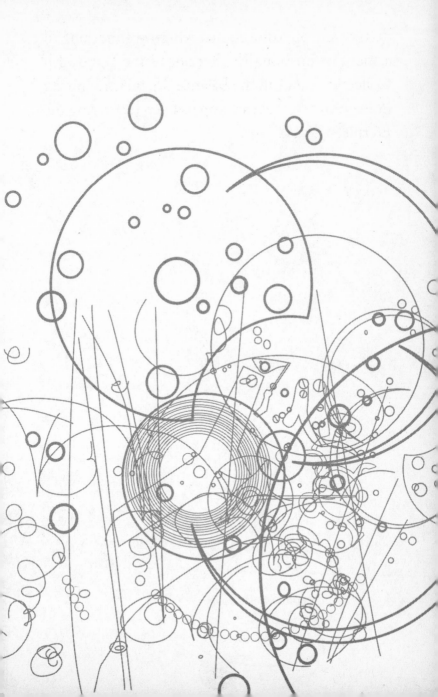

The Way to Dusty Death

The dust was getting thicker. It seemed to be seeping into the corridor, gathering and forming into shapes. The Doctor grabbed Lisa.

'Help Henderson,' he shouted to Bobby. 'And run!'

Bobby helped the engineer to his feet and they hurried after the Doctor and Lisa, who were disappearing into the fog of dust. Henderson was still groggy and needed Bobby's help after his ordeal in the generator room.

The dust was dry and Bobby could feel it coating her clothes, her skin, the back of her throat. She kept her eyes almost closed as they ran. An arm, formed from the grey dirt, thrust out in front of them. Bobby ignored it and kept running. She felt the impact as it caught her across the chest. The arm exploded into powder, and she kept running.

At the end of the corridor, the Doctor was waiting with Lisa. The girl looked almost unconscious as the Doctor held her up.

'We can't hang around,' the Doctor said. 'It'll be after us soon.'

'But what is it?' Henderson asked. He coughed with the effort.

'Is it alive?' Bobby asked.

'Certainly seems it. Living dust,' the Doctor pulled a face. 'Not something you see every day. Which is probably just as well, really.' He tightened his grip on Lisa. 'Right, come on then.'

Bobby shouted into her radio as they ran. 'Clinton – Clinton, can you hear me?' But the only reply was static.

Or was it? She could just about make out the broken sound of a voice, beneath the sound of the static, the pounding of her heart and the rasps of her breath as she ran.

'Clinton? Are you there? I can't hear you.'

'Here, let me.' The Doctor took the radio from her as they struggled onwards. The floor was coated with dust that swirled and clawed at their feet as they ran.

'If you can hear me, Clinton,' the Doctor yelled into the radio, 'track this signal. We're all together, but we've got trouble. Can you close the sections behind us? Seal them off. And turn the air conditioning and ventilation up to maximum where we are. Blow as much air through as you can.'

The static might have been a voice. It might have been Clinton's reply. It was impossible to tell, so the Doctor handed the radio back to Bobby, and they kept going.

Lisa and Henderson had recovered enough now that they didn't need helping along. But they weren't up to running. The most they could manage was a stumbling jog.

'You think anyone heard?' Lisa gasped.

As she spoke, a metal shutter closed behind them, blocking the corridor and cutting off the sight of the grey figures lurching after them.

The dust on the floor was whipped up angrily. It seemed to sense it was alone now, and clawed and tore at their feet. Ahead of them, the whole floor was rippling as the dust drew up into a curtain across the corridor. Arms thrust out through it, snatching at the heavy air, waiting for the

Doctor and his friends to get close enough for it to grab them.

'We're trapped,' Henderson realized.

'Come on, Clinton,' the Doctor said quietly. 'I know you heard me. Where's that air conditioning?'

The first sign was the hiss of the air blowing in through vents in the walls close to the floor. Then the curtain of dust began to sway. It struggled to keep together, but soon the air rushing along the corridor was tearing holes in the creature. For a moment a face formed in the ragged sheet across the corridor. A mouth twisted and screamed in anger.

Then the whole curtain was torn apart, dust blasting down the corridor as the raging wind blew it to pieces.

'Time to go!' the Doctor shouted above the gale.

They set off again, the wind whipping at their clothes and their hair.

With the power back on, the security cameras were working. Clinton and Professor Dollund stared at the screens above the main control console. But most of them showed only a grey mist – dust hanging in the air in front of the cameras.

'I think that's them,' Dollund said, pointing

to one of the screens. Vague, dark shapes were hurrying past, close to the camera.

'I hope you're right,' Clinton replied, operating the controls that would seal off the section of corridor behind the fleeing figures.

The intercom crackled and popped, but it was impossible to make out what anyone at the other end might be saying.

'We should keep this door sealed, until they get here,' Dollund said.

'Good idea.' Clinton pressed a button, and the main door slid closed.

The slight breeze caused by the movement made the thin coating of dust across the floor shiver and ripple. But neither Clinton nor Professor Dollund noticed…

The Doctor skidded on the dusty floor and crashed into the closed door to the main control room. Henderson and Lisa were able to run without help now, and Bobby brought up the rear.

The Doctor knocked hard on the door. 'Come on, come on.' He glanced nervously over his shoulder. A wave of the grey dust was sweeping through the corridor, filling it with choking particles that rushed towards them.

'What are you doing in there?' the Doctor yelled. 'Let us in!'

Professor Dollund's voice was muffled. 'How do we know it's you?'

'Well who else would it be – the milkman?'

'Open the door!' Bobby shouted, hammering on it with her fists. 'Quickly!'

Slowly, as if reluctant, the door slid open. As soon as the gap was wide enough, the Doctor pushed Bobby through, then Lisa and finally Henderson. Then he jumped through himself.

'Shut it, shut it!' he shouted.

'I don't know – open it, close it…' Clinton muttered. But he operated the controls and the door slid closed again, just as a wave of dust crashed against it.

A fine mist sprayed through the last millimetres of the gap between the door and its frame and scattered across the control room floor.

The Doctor was immediately at the control console with Clinton. 'Have you sent the distress signal?'

'I don't know, to be honest.' Clinton pointed to one of the readout screens. 'I've sent the message, but I'm not getting a confirmation that it's actually gone out. This whole system is clogged with dust. Goodness only knows how much of it is actually working. We're lucky to have life support and gravity.'

'At least we should be safe in here,' Lisa said. She was sitting on the floor, breathing heavily.

Henderson slumped down beside her. 'I didn't think we were ever going to get here. That dust – what is it?'

The Doctor whistled through his teeth as he considered. 'Just dust, I think. But it's been animated by some controlling force. Something that binds it together and which obviously has an agenda.'

'What sort of agenda?' Dollund wondered. 'You mean it knows we're here? It wants something?'

'Probably not as conscious or deliberate as that. Maybe it just sees us as a threat. Maybe it's just trying to survive.'

'I know the feeling,' Clinton grumbled. He brushed away dust from the control console with the back of his hand.

'Doctor,' Bobby said quietly. 'I think we have a problem.'

She pointed at the door. It was bulging inwards, the metal rippling and denting as something incredibly strong tried to force its way inside. The edge of the door was pushed clear of the frame. Dust was pouring through like sand falling down the narrow neck of an hourglass.

'That doesn't look good,' the Doctor agreed. 'Clinton, can you seal the doorway with a forceshield, make it airtight?'

But Clinton didn't answer.

The dust he had been brushing absent-mindedly off the control panel had gathered itself into a pile on the floor. A pile that coalesced into a distinct shape. A shape that became a hand and had launched itself at Clinton.

The dusty grey fingers clamped on his throat, the palm smothering over his mouth as Clinton fought for breath and tried desperately to wrench the hand away from his neck.

The dust falling through the door was rising up too – forming into a lumpy, misshapen figure that reached out with its death-grey hands as it lurched across the room.

Crystal Clear

Bobby immediately ran to help Clinton. The hand was clamped on his throat. Bobby could feel her own fingers sinking into the surface as she tried to prise it away – just as her feet sank into the dust on the lunar surface…

The grey, misshapen creature formed from the dust that had spilled in through the doorway was reaching for the Doctor. As she struggled to help Clinton, Bobby saw Henderson pick up one of the chairs beside the main console and swing it in a low arc at the grey creature.

The chair connected, and kept going. The creature exploded into grey particles – dust floating gently down through the air.

But almost at once another creature was forming. And yet another was forcing its way through the ever-increasing gap between the door and its frame. The corridor outside was filled with dust, hanging heavily like smoke in the air.

Finally, the pressure of Bobby and Clinton's combined grip on the hand crushed it. The whole thing shattered into dust and drifted like mist to join the particles that were already reforming into another lumpy, grotesque creature.

Lisa gave a shriek as a fist of dust smashed towards her. The Doctor raised his sonic screwdriver. The tip glowed blue and there was a high-pitched, whirring sound. The fist exploded.

'Sounds like I got the right frequency,' the Doctor said grimly.

'But you can't stop them all like that,' Professor Dollund gasped. He was swinging a clipboard in front of him, driving back a haze of dust. But the dust was clawing round his hands, dragging at the clipboard, ripping it away.

The creature in the doorway seemed to grow thinner to squeeze through, filling out again as it entered the control room. At its neck, the Crystal they had all seen in the cavern caught the light and sparkled with inner fire.

'That Crystal,' Bobby gasped.

'I see it,' the Doctor said.

'What about it?' Henderson said. He was still swinging the chair for all he was worth, but he seemed to be tiring.

Clinton and Bobby were backing away from the console. The dust in the air in front of them was coalescing, forming into the hand again. Its powdery fingers probed the air as it sought them out.

'Never mind the Crystal,' Clinton shouted. 'Just get those things… that stuff out of here.'

'Don't you see?' the Doctor said, fiddling with his sonic screwdriver. 'The Crystal is the key. It's the Crystal that's animating the dust.'

'That's ridiculous,' Dollund snapped.

'Oh, you think?' The Doctor held up the sonic screwdriver. It glowed and whirred, but the lumpy grey creature with the Crystal at its neck lumbered forwards unaffected.

'What are you doing, Doctor?' Lisa asked, dodging out of the way of a dusty arm that snatched at her.

'Wasting time,' Dollund said.

'Saving your lives,' the Doctor snapped back. 'If I can't find a frequency that interferes with whatever signals that Crystal is giving out to animate this dust…' He tried the sonic screwdriver again. Still there was no effect. 'Then we're all dead,' the Doctor finished grimly.

The grey creature lurched onwards. Its hands reached out for the Doctor, closing on his neck. The sonic screwdriver was knocked from his hands and skidded across the floor…

A supra-lightspeed shuttle pod had been prepared. The robot Agent only just fitted inside the sleek capsule.

'We need only the final coordinates,' Sister Maggen told Drakon. 'The pod can reach any point in this galaxy mere moments after it is launched.'

Drakon nodded his approval, the shadows beneath his hood deepening as he lowered his head. 'We are so very close,' he rasped. 'Brother Ardos will have the coordinates very soon.'

'Does he know why the Crystal has become active again?' Sister Maggen wondered.

'No one knows,' Drakon told her. 'Except perhaps the traitor Varlos. He fashioned the Crystal, created it out of the raw stuff of the universe. Only he truly understands it.'

'If we find the Crystal, we may find Varlos,' Sister Maggen said.

'Yes,' Drakon agreed. 'And if we do…' His husky voice tailed off. 'But it is the Crystal that must be our first priority. The Agent understands that.' He turned to the robot standing inside the egg-like pod. 'You know what you must do?'

The robot's head inclined slightly. Its voice was an echoing metallic boom. 'My mission parameters are defined. Priorities have been set out. Failure is not an option.'

'Excellent,' Drakon said quietly. 'With such technology, such expertise, such ruthless determination, the Darksmiths of Karagula cannot fail!'

Another cloaked and hooded Darksmith hurried into the chamber. Drakon turned to greet him. 'Brother Ardos, you have news?'

'Yes, High Minister,' Ardos said. 'The Crystal has increased its signal. We now have an exact position. I have fed the coordinates into the main network and the pod is being programmed with its course trajectory.'

Drakon moved to inspect a screen set into the inner shell of the pod door. A stream of numbers and symbols scrolled rapidly across it, reflecting in the pale gelatinous flesh of Drakon's skull-like face.

'Lunar 1 of Sol 3 in the Mutter's Spiral,' Drakon said. 'A moon orbiting a planet known as…' He peered at the screen. 'Terra.'

'More commonly called "Earth", High Minister,' Ardos said. 'Although the planet is heavily populated, its Moon is uninhabited except for some scientific and geological teams, it would seem.'

'That doesn't matter,' Drakon told him. But his words were also meant for the armoured robot standing patiently inside the pod. 'Whatever it takes, we must have the Crystal. No matter how many people have to die in the process.'

There was a bleep from the pod. The door swung heavily shut, cutting off the Darksmiths' view of their creation.

'I understand.' The voice was muffled through the shell of the pod. 'I am ready.'

The Darksmiths drew back, walking quickly and silently to the back of the chamber where huge blast screens had been erected. From behind them, Drakon, Ardos, Maggen and her assistants watched through thick windows of toughened duraglass.

Sister Maggen was standing at a small control console that, like the screen, seemed to have been carved from stone. She reached for a control, and the roof of the chamber slid open. Above the vaulted dome stars shone down from a cloudless sky.

Then the chamber echoed with the sound of the pod's powerful supra-lightspeed engines. The pod shivered for a moment, fire erupting from beneath it. There was a tremendous flash of light. Drakon and the others shielded their sensitive eyes with their translucent hands. The bones of their fingers were silhouetted against the light for a moment. Then it was gone.

And the pod was gone too. A tiny streak of fire etched across the heavens, heading for a distant star, a small blue planet, a grey dusty moon…

Dust to Dust

The Doctor hurled himself aside as the grey hands reached for him. He felt the dusty dry limbs brush across his face and grab at him as he fell. His shoulder hit the floor hard, forcing a cry from his lips as he skidded across the dusty floor.

The floor itself was alive, clawing at his clothes, trying to hold him down. He rolled on to his stomach and scrabbled onwards. He could see the sonic screwdriver ahead of him, and he stretched out, desperate to reach it.

Henderson swung the chair again, sending the dust flying. But he was being forced back into a corner of the room. His foot caught on something and he stumbled, almost falling.

The sonic screwdriver was kicked out of the Doctor's reach. He gave a grunt of annoyance and frustration and heaved himself after it. The dust was still dragging him down. Tiny claws ripped at him, holding him back.

Then a massive grey foot stamped down inches from the Doctor's face. He rolled desperately away. The foot stamped again. Grey arms reached down. Darkness closed over his face. The Doctor was fighting, thumping, tearing at the powdery hands that held him. He could taste the dust, could feel it forcing its way into his mouth, choking him.

'This what you want?' a voice said. It was muffled and filtered by the dust that enveloped the Doctor's head.

He felt something being pressed into his hand. The sonic screwdriver. He plunged it into the grey fog that surrounded him. Heard the faint sound of the sonic beam. Then he was breathing again, the dust was gone and Bobby was kneeling beside him, smiling with relief.

The Doctor smiled a thank you. But there was no time for anything more, not yet. He leaped to his feet and stood facing the grey dust monster that was lumbering heavily towards him. Dust swirled round its feet like mist. The Crystal at its thick neck sparkled and glowed with icy fire.

The glow of the sonic screwdriver was just as bright. The whole room seemed to shake with the high-pitched sound it gave off.

Clinton and Henderson were backed into a corner, pummelling the heavy air with their bare hands. Professor Dollund was crouched beside the main console, trying to shield Lisa who was curled in a protective ball on the ground behind him. Bobby stood beside the Doctor, facing down the monster.

The grey creature hesitated. Then it took another step forward. But its foot didn't stop when it met the floor. It was like it was taking a step down a flight of stairs. The crude lumpy features of the creature's face twisted in surprise and fear. Then its other leg collapsed too, dust shooting out from it and scattering across the floor.

The thing pitched slowly forwards on to its face. It hit the floor, and exploded into particles. A cloud of dust billowed upwards.

Coughing, the Doctor waved the dust away. He stepped into the mist, reached down, and picked up the heavy Crystal that lay in a pile of inanimate dust on the floor.

It glowed weakly in his palm for a moment.

Then the light died away, and was gone.

The Doctor tossed the Crystal into the air, caught it and pushed it into his jacket pocket. 'There you go,' he said. 'Wave cancellation. Should sort it out, at least for a while. Until I can get it into a stasis casket.'

He looked round the control room. He watched Dollund and Lisa getting slowly to their feet, Clinton and Henderson looking round the wrecked room in surprise and relief. He let Bobby hug him tight, and laughed. The room around them was deep with dust and dirt.

'I think,' the Doctor said, 'that you need a decent cleaning woman. Or man. Or Snorkellian. Great cleaners the Snorkellians, suck up the dust and dirt through those big snouts and digest it. Ends up as handy little pellets that are great for growing tomatoes.' He frowned as a thought struck him. 'Not sure I actually like tomatoes,' he said slowly. 'Still never mind. Ashes to ashes.' He kicked listlessly at the floor. 'Dust to dust.'

'We have a problem, High Minister,' Brother Ardos said.

Drakon turned slowly towards him. He was

standing in the main debating chamber of the Darksmiths, preparing to deliver a report to the members of the Witan, the Darksmiths' ruling council.

'Problem?' Drakon echoed. The veins in his translucent face pulsed angrily.

'The Eternity Crystal. It has… stopped.' Ardos bowed his head, expecting the worst.

But Drakon's voice was quiet and controlled. 'Stopped? What do you mean?'

'I am sorry…'

'What do you mean?' Drakon repeated, louder. This time there was no mistaking the edge of anger and irritation in his voice.

'We are no longer detecting its emissions.'

'Has it moved out of range?'

'No, High Minister. It was there, and then it was gone. It didn't move from Earth's Moon. The emissions have stopped.'

'You mean they have reduced to the faint trace we could detect before? Enough to know the Crystal still exists, but not enough to trace its whereabouts?'

'No, High Minister,' Ardos said nervously. 'Not even that. Nothing. Nothing at all.'

There was silence for several moments. 'That is not possible,' Drakon said. 'Only Varlos knows how to destroy the Crystal. No one can stop its wave emissions entirely, unless…'

'High Minister?'

Drakon's voice was quiet but determined.

'Can we get a message to the Agent?'

Ardos nodded. 'We can still despatch a message capsule that will reach the pod before the Agent arrives on Earth's Moon, yes. But it must be soon.'

'Then tell the Agent that it is facing a powerful enemy. Someone with the knowledge to block the Crystal's emissions. Tell the Agent that nothing must stand in its way. If it has to use extreme force, then so be it. We must have the Eternity Crystal, whatever the cost.'

Ardos bowed and hurried from the chamber. He had created the Agent, and he knew what 'extreme force' it was capable of. Whoever had taken the Crystal would soon be dead.

Sentence of Death

The stasis casket looked like a fairly ordinary small metal box, not much bigger than the Crystal itself. A swirling circular pattern was embossed on to the dull metal. The Doctor took a last look at the beautiful Crystal resting on the purple velvet inside, then closed the lid of the stasis casket. A simple clasp held the box shut. The Doctor balanced the box on the TARDIS console. He was sure it was this Crystal that had somehow drawn the TARDIS to the Moon. It must be incredibly powerful.

Inside the casket, the Crystal could signal or transmit, or emit waves or resonate or do whatever it liked, but none of it would leave the box. It was completely sealed. The inside, as far as the rest of the universe was concerned, did not exist.

The Doctor's next task was to send for help. He opened a communications channel through the TARDIS' systems and sent the coded message that Clinton had recorded for him. The main communications in the base were so clogged with dust – even dry, dead, ordinary dust as it now was, that they didn't work and would take an age to repair. Quicker to use the TARDIS, and he could see that the Crystal was kept safe at the same time.

The Doctor's hand hesitated over the main lever. He was about to leave the Moon. There was help on the way, and the Crystal intrigued him – he'd like some time to examine it properly and safely. Some time to work out who had made it, and why...

But then again, he owed it to his new friends to check they were all right and to tell them that help was on the way. He couldn't send them a message any more than they could signal out of the base. A few minutes, just to make sure everything was hunky dory, tickety-boo, going swimmingly...

Before he went, he attached a set of cables to sockets on the outside of the stasis casket. No reason why the TARDIS shouldn't start analysing it without him.

TARDIS
Data Bank
Analysis of Crystal

Crystal — from the Greek 'krynos', meaning 'icy cold'.
This is because people used to believe that natural crystals were
made of ice that had frozen so hard it couldn't thaw.
There are seven types of crystal, grouped by the type of symmetry:

- ✧ **Monoclinic** (most common)
- ✧ **Triclinic**
- ✧ **Cubic**
- ✧ **Hexagonal**
- ✧ **Tetragonal**
- ✧ **Orthorhombic**
- ✧ **Rhombohedral** (also known as Trigonal)

No two crystals are ever exactly alike, as the conditions in which they are grown always vary, even if only slightly.

This Crystal is a perfect form of Hexagonal crystal with an unidentified internal power supply that creates a resonance similar to the vibration qualities of quartz, but it is also as hard as diamond.

Analysis shows that this Crystal was deliberately constructed for a specific purpose. But there is no way of knowing who made it, or what they intended to use it for...

Professor Dollund shook the Doctor's hand enthusiastically. 'It's been very enlightening, Doctor,' he said.

'Oh for me too,' the Doctor assured him. 'Enlightening, uplifting, enthralling, and a bit dangerous.' He grinned. 'Just how I like it.'

Henderson and Clinton shook the Doctor's hand too. 'Thanks,' Henderson said, 'for everything.'

'Oh, it was nothing. Well, maybe something, but nothing much. Not really.'

'Good to meet you, Doctor,' Clinton said. 'Sorry it got so hectic.'

'Did it?' the Doctor shrugged. 'Always does when I'm around.'

Lisa gave the Doctor a quick hug. 'Thanks,' she said quietly.

'Pleasure,' the Doctor said, just as quietly.

Then he was almost knocked flying as Bobby pulled him into a tight embrace. 'Careful,' the Doctor said, winded. 'I might break.'

'Not you,' Bobby said tearfully.

'No, well, maybe not,' the Doctor admitted. 'You look after yourself,' he told her. 'Help's on the way, won't be long now.'

'Moon Buggies are here already,' Clinton

announced. 'Er,' he went on, 'actually Doctor, you might want to get back up top pretty quickly. One of the relief crews is loading your blue box thing on to a Buggy. Looks like they're taking it back with them.' He turned to the Doctor. 'Is that all right?'

But the Doctor had gone.

By the time he emerged on to the Moon's surface again, the TARDIS was gone. Two Moon Buggies had stopped inside the forceshield bubble that Clinton had put up. The Moon Buggies were large white vehicles with huge rubber tyres that sank into the lunar dust. The cabin was a bulbous dome at the end of a long, thin deck on which cargo, like the TARDIS, could be loaded.

There were several sets of tyre tracks showing where other Moon Buggies had been and gone. One of them had taken the TARDIS, but which one?

Activity

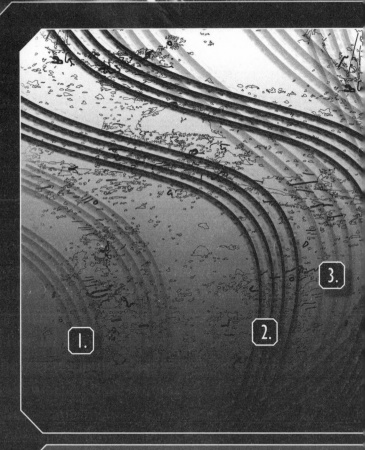

The Doctor examined the tracks for any clue as to which Moon Buggy had taken the TARDIS.

4.

5.

6.

Answer:

After a quick examination, the Doctor climbed up into the protective airtight dome of the nearest Buggy. He flashed his psychic paper at the driver sitting inside.

'Customs and Excise, blue box division,' he said. 'Follow those tracks.' He pointed to the set of tracks he was sure were left by the Buggy that was carrying the TARDIS.

'Right you are, sir,' the driver replied. The Moon Buggy set off, a cloud of dust blown up like smoke behind it.

Soon the low angular buildings of the main spaceport came into view on the horizon.

'How did you know which tracks to follow?' the driver asked. 'They all look the same to me.'

'One set was deeper,' the Doctor explained. 'So that was the Buggy carrying the heaviest load. The blue box I'm after isn't exactly light, so I'm betting it's on that Buggy.'

The driver nodded. 'Seems fair enough. Looks like the Buggy went into Hangar 7. I'll drop you there and get back to work if that's OK?'

Hangar 7 was a vast open space. Standing alone and abandoned inside the hangar was a Moon

Buggy. The Doctor smiled with delight. But as he approached, the smile faded to a frown. The Buggy's cargo deck was empty.

The Doctor could see the dusty outline where something had been standing – something square and the exact size of the TARDIS. But it had gone now. The Doctor looked round, hoping to see someone he could ask where the TARDIS had been taken.

There was only one figure in sight. A robot built of metal and plastic. It walked with an elegance and speed that was surprising.

'Oh, hi,' the Doctor said as the robot approached. 'Look at you, someone took pride in their work, didn't they. You are beautiful, you know that? What engineering. What design. What – *are you doing*?!'

The Doctor's voice had become a strangled yelp as the robot hauled him off his feet. It lifted the Doctor into the air, then hurled him aside. The Doctor crashed painfully into the Moon Buggy, and slumped to the ground. He shook his head groggily, wondering what was going on. 'Was it something I said?' he muttered.

The robot was looming over him. Metal fingers snapped viciously as it reached down for the

Doctor. Its voice was an echoing metallic boom.

'Brother Varlos – I have found you at last,' it grated. 'You have been tried in your absence, and sentenced to death.'

To Be Continued...

To find out what events lie in store
for the Doctor and the mystery of the
Darksmith Legacy, look out for
The Graves of Mordane.
But for now, here is a taste of
things to come...

DOCTOR · WHO

BBC

Book
2

THE **DARKSMITH** LEGACY
THE GRAVES OF MORDANE

BY COLIN BRAKE

www.thedarksmithlegacy.com
Continue the amazing adventure online...

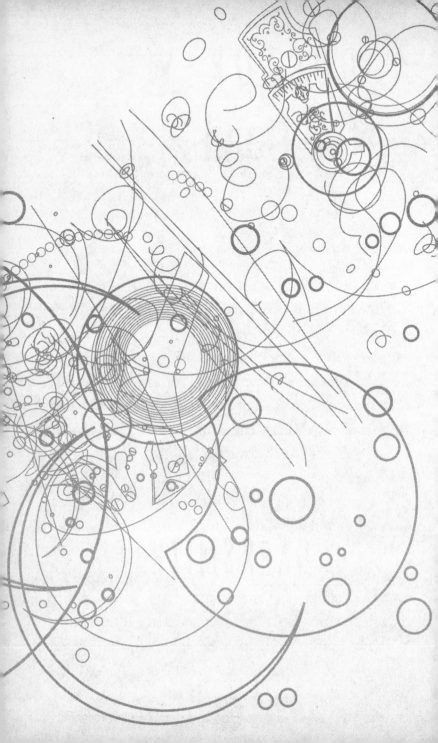

The Dead Planet

In a distant galaxy on the planet Mordane, three brave humans were walking through the biggest cemetery in known space. Mordane was, literally, a planet of the dead. It had been used for centuries by the space-faring peoples of a thousand worlds. The entire surface of the planet was covered by cemeteries and catacombs, the final resting place for the much loved dead of over a hundred different species.

'I suppose at least we know now why the planet was declared off limits,' said the youngest of the party, a pretty girl of about sixteen who liked to be called Catz, although her real name was Caroline.

The eldest of the group, a tough-looking women with a well-lined face snorted with derision. 'That's going to help me sleep at night!' she commented sarcastically and stomped ahead.

'Don't worry about Captain Gomez,' first officer Chandra told the young girl sympathetically. 'She just wants to find what we need so we can get off this place.'

The three of them continued in silence, moving between the long rows of gravestones towards the mausolea ahead of them. This was Sector Alpha, on the continent given over to human remains.

As well as thousands and thousands of regular graves there were also numerous family mausolea and catacombs in which thousands of other dead humans were enjoying the endless sleep of death. Except, as Captain Gomez and her two companions had discovered when their ship had crashed here two days ago, the 'sleep' was not as endless as they had been led to believe.

'We need to make camp,' announced the Captain. Chandra nodded and slipped his heavy rucksack from his back. Catz watched as the rucksack expanded, on command, unfolding itself into a massive tent that secured itself to the ground and to nearby gravestones. The plastic looked flimsy but Catz knew that when the right signal was activated it would solidify into a protective shell that would keep out any hostile forces. This was the third night that she would be grateful for the protection of the Intelligent Plastic Survival Pod.

'It's nearly dark,' Chandra told her. 'Get inside before it starts.'

Catz clambered into the tent, and Chandra followed her. She looked behind her to see Captain Gomez staring back at the sinking sun.

'Can you see anything Captain?' asked Chandra. Gomez nodded and then turned and hurried to join them inside the tent. Chandra operated the sonic control and the door sealed itself. Gomez looked at her two companions with a serious expression.

'It's starting,' she told them.

DOCTOR · WHO

Fantastic free Doctor Who slipcase offer when you buy two Darksmith Legacy books!

Limited to the first 500 respondents!

To be eligible to receive your free slipcase, fill in your details on the form below and send along with original receipt(s) showing the purchase of two Darksmith Legacy books. The first 500 correctly completed forms will receive a slipcase.

Offer subject to availability. Terms and conditions apply. See overleaf for details.

Here

Entry Form

Name: ....

Address: ....

Email: ....

Have you remembered to include your two original sales receipts? ⬡

I have read and agree to the terms and conditions overleaf. ⬡

Tick here if you don't want to receive marketing communications from Penguin Brands and Licensing. ⬡

Important – Are you over 13 years old?

If you are 13 or over just tick this box, you don't need to do anything else. ⬡

If you are under 13, you must get your parent or guardian to enter the promotion on your behalf. If they agree, please show them the notice below.

Notice to parent/guardian of entrants under 13 years old

If you are a parent/guardian of the entrant and you consent to the retention and use of the entrant's personal details by Penguin Brands and Licensing for the purposes of this promotion, please tick this box. ⬡

Name of parent/guardian: ....

Terms and Conditions

1. This promotion is subject to availability and is limited to the first 500 correctly completed respondents received.
2. This promotion is open to all residents aged 7 years or over in the UK, with the exception of employees of the Promoter, their immediate families and anyone else connected with this promotion. Entries from entrants under the age of 13 years must be made by a parent/guardian on their behalf.
3. The Promoter accepts no responsibility for any entries that are incomplete, illegal or fail to reach the promoter for any reason. Proof of sending is not proof of receipt. Entries via agents or third parties are invalid.
4. Only one entry per person. No entrant may receive more than one slipcase.
5. To enter, fill in your details on the entry form and send along with original sales receipt(s) showing purchase of two Doctor Who: The Darksmith Legacy books to: Doctor Who Slipcase Offer, Brands and Licensing, 80 Strand, London, WC2R 0RL.
6. The first 500 correctly completed entries will receive a slipcase.
7. Offer only available on purchases of Doctor Who: The Darksmith Legacy books.
8. Please allow 31days for receipt of your slip case.
9. Slip cases are subject to availability. In the event of exceptional circumstances, the Promoter reserves the right to amend or foreclose the promotion without notice. No correspondence will be entered into.
10. All instructions given on the entry form, form part of the terms and conditions.
11. The Promoter will use any data submitted by entrants for only the purposes of running the promotion, unless otherwise stated in the entry details. By entering this promotion, all entrants consent to the use of their personal data by the Promoter for the purposes of the administration of this promotion and any other purposes to which the entrant has consented.
12. By entering this promotion, each entrant agrees to be bound by these terms and conditions.
13. The Promoter is Penguin Books Limited, 80 Strand, London WC2R 0RL.

Cut Here ---------------------------------

Doctor Who Slipcase Offer

Brands and Licensing

80 Strand

London

WC2R 0RL